THE HENCHMAN'S OBSESSION

ENDLESS OBSESSION

SADIE KING

THE HENCHMAN'S OBSESSION

He'll risk everything for his one obsession...

The moment I saw her photograph, my life changed.

Her image, forever etched into my brain.

Mine.

It's all I can think as I track her down, scouring the county for my boss's daughter.

He thinks I'm bringing her home, but her home is with me now.

She wants a quiet life. I'll give it to her.

I'll be the wholesome small-town man if that's what she wants. I'll be anything she needs me to be.

But she must never know that I work for her father...

The Henchman's Obsession is a soft stalker romance featuring an OTT alpha male and the curvy woman he claims as his own.

PROLOGUE

They call him a lot of things: heartless, poverty maker, the most hated man on the Sunset Coast. But they hardly ever call him Father.

The worn-looking man sitting behind the mahogany desk in a rumpled shirt with dark shadows under his eyes and a hand that trembles as he reaches for his whiskey glass is what most people don't see. Damon Fletcher—the father who's been broken by the disappearance of his daughters.

"She ran away three days ago, right after her sister."

I steal a glance at the man standing next to me, wondering why we've both been called in to hear this news.

I've not seen him before, but then again I don't know all of Damon's crew down the coast.

The one standing next to me is a huge brick of a man, with shoulders even wider than mine, a thickset jaw, eyes like pools of darkness, and a stillness about him that's unnerving.

He's staring straight ahead, his face passive, unmoved by the display of fatherly distress in front of us.

I've been working for Damon for six years, and I've never seen him like this.

My expertise lies in managing his interests further up the coast, doing what's necessary to keep his interests running and profitable.

Yesterday he called me down to the Sunset Coast to see him. It's not often I get called in by the boss.

"You think they're together?" I ask.

Damon brings the whiskey glass to his lips, takes a sip, then knocks it down in one gulp. His mouth puckers briefly, then he smacks his lips.

"No."

Being located up the coast, I've never met Damon's family, but I hear he's got two spoiled brats for daughters.

"Chastity will be fine." He sets his tumbler on the table and leans back in his chair. "But Trinity…"

Damon's eyes go misty, and for a frightful moment I think he's going to cry. I look at the beefcake next to me, but he's not giving anything away, the hardnosed bastard.

"Chastity is independent. She can look after herself. But Trinity is a sensitive soul. The thought of her being out there alone…"

He trails off, unable to go on.

It's hard to keep the irritation from my expression. She's probably partying it up with some preppy kid, spending her allowance on cocktails and tequila shots.

But I don't let the boss see what I'm thinking. No way.

"I'm sorry, sir."

"I want you to find her."

He leans on the table, and his eyes are suddenly sharp. His beady gaze lingers on mine and then shifts to the lump of man next to me.

I dig my nails into my palms, hoping he can't see my knuckles turning white. It doesn't pay to get angry with the boss. But I am angry. I've been brought down here away from my work to find some runaway rich girl who's probably shacked up with a trust fund baby enjoying a few days of freedom.

"Why us?"

I keep my voice steady, hoping I don't sound too petulant, but I feel fucking petulant. I'm a hard negotiator. I've got good business sense. Yet I'm being put to use tracking down a runaway. Not the best use of my skills.

"Because she doesn't know either of you."

Great. The out of town dudes get to do the babysitting. Beefcake still isn't saying anything, and I wonder if he's as pissed about this as I am.

"You think she doesn't want to be found?"

"I know she doesn't. She left this note."

Damon pulls a scribbled piece of paper out of a folder and lays it on the table. The writing is cursive, pretty with feminine curls to the letters.

I want a different life.

Don't try to find me.

Sorry, Daddy.

I wonder how long she'll last when she finds out that a different life doesn't involve all expenses paid by Daddy.

"Can't you track her credit card?" I ask.

"She didn't take it."

That surprises me. A rich-girl runaway isn't going to get far with no money.

"She withdrew a thousand dollars from the bank and left her card with the note. She could be anywhere."

Maybe she's found herself a sugar daddy to pay her way and give her the luxuries that I'm sure Damon's family must be used to.

I keep my thoughts to myself because suggesting to the boss that his daughter is likely hooking up with a rich older man who's demanding God knows what favors to keep her in luxury is likely to get me killed.

"I want you to work together to find her and bring her home."

"I work alone."

So, the beefcake speaks. The hard-ass next to me is staring intently at Damon. I don't like the thought of working with this guy either. I doubt there'd be many laughs with someone who has a permanent don't-fuck-with-me look etched on his face.

"That's fine with me. If you've got it covered, I'm not needed."

I raise my hands as if to concede, but Damon turns his gaze to me.

"Not so fast. Sting is an excellent tracker, but this requires a bit more sensitivity than what he's used to."

My mind reels at the name. Sting. The man's got quite a reputation.

The right hand of Damon. The man who does the deeds Damon doesn't want to dirty his hands with. There's a joke amongst us henchmen that if you go against the boss, he'll send Sting for you. The guy's a hitman.

"I work alone."

Sting says it again as if Damon hasn't just spoken. His voice chills me. No sane father would send this man after his little girl.

But when has Damon Fletcher ever been sane?

"You work together."

Damon counters Sting casually as if he's a wayward child that needs pulling into line and not a massive fucking scary as shit hitman.

Sting still doesn't move, and I wonder if that's something he learned in hitman training, how to stay really fucking still and freak everyone the fuck out.

Damon pulls a photo out of his folder and throws it on the table.

"This is Trinity."

My gaze goes to the image, and my heart stops. There's a ringing in my ears, and everything blurs around me, except that photo.

The picture's taken on a boat, the family yacht no doubt. A young woman, Trinity, sits side-on to the camera, her shoulders twisted frontward, laughing at something just out of frame.

She's wearing a sheer wrap thrown over her bikini-clad shoulders, the lines of her cleavage visible under the fabric. Her head's thrown back in a laugh that shows off plump lips, straight teeth, and her pink tongue poking over her bottom teeth. Smile lines draw attention to her sparkling eyes that are the same color as the water around the boat.

Her neck is elongated, and there's a sprinkling of freckles on her nose and throat.

She's beautiful, more than beautiful. There's a pull to her, a stirring in my gut telling me that this woman is my destiny.

Mine.

A possessiveness grabs my heart, and I know without a doubt that my life will never be the same again.

Damon's talking, but I don't hear what he's saying. My eyes are transfixed on Trinity's face, committing it to memory. Her image is branded into my heart.

Mine.

The world swims around my mind, and I feel dizzy. I need to find this woman. For my own sanity, I need to find her and make her mine.

"I'll find her." My voice comes out as a croak. "I don't need Sting."

Damon peers at me, and I wonder if he can sense what just happened, how my whole world just shifted.

"I'll do it alone."

Damon looks between us, exasperated like we're his naughty children who won't play ball. But Sting only works alone, and I don't want anyone cramping my style.

"Fine," he says. "Find her, Karl. Find her and bring her home."

"Yes, sir."

I'll find her, all right. I'll bring her home. Home to me, where she belongs.

TRINITY

The man in front of the counter jiggles his keys nervously.

"I'm sure she'll love them." I give him a reassuring smile as I wrap string around the bouquet of long stem roses.

"Do you think so?"

He seems nervous, and I wonder if they're for a new love or someone he's trying to make up to. Or maybe he just wants to surprise his girlfriend.

"It's a bit cliché, isn't it? Red roses."

It must be a new girlfriend or a first date that he wants to impress.

The man wipes a bead of sweat from his forehead, and I notice the gold band. So, he's either really trying to make up to his wife or he's got a mistress.

I snip the string and lay the roses on the table.

There's a pot of small heart-shaped chocolates wrapped in tin foil, and I'm supposed to add a few into the wrapping of the flowers for our romantic customers, but if these roses are for his mistress, then he doesn't deserve chocolates to go with them.

"I'm sure she'll like them." My voice comes out clipped.

"They're for my wife, Brook," he says, picking the roses up off the counter. "It's our wedding anniversary, and she's been working so hard with the kids, and all the dogs…"

He trails off, making me wonder just how many dogs one family needs.

"We own the dog hotel," he clarifies. "She never gets any time off. I just want it to be really special for her."

They're for his wife. I relax. He is one of the good guys.

"I'm taking her away for the weekend. She doesn't know anything about it. I'm nervous that I've got it wrong, you know?"

I nod sympathetically. "I'm sure she'll love it."

He's about to go when I dig my hand into the pot of chocolates. "Here, take some of these. Sweeten the deal."

"Thank you."

The man beams at me, and I wonder how I ever thought he was an adulterer.

It's a bad habit. Since I started working at Beautiful Blossoms two weeks ago, I've been trying to guess the backstories of my customers. Who they're buying flowers for, what their relationship to the person is, what the occasion is, or what they're trying to make up for.

The man leaves the shop, and I tidy up the counter, sweeping the rose stems into the bin and making sure the cellophane and string are put back neatly. Any mess in the shop could set off Aria's anxiety.

Aria co-owns Beautiful Blossoms and has taken me under her wing since I stepped off a Greyhound bus to stretch my legs and saw a help wanted sign on the bus station noticeboard two weeks ago.

The jingle of the shop bell makes me look up, and I smile to see Jenny coming in with baby Aurora pinned to her chest.

"She's out back." I indicate the back room where Jenny's best friend and business partner, Aria, is doing the inventory.

The baby stirs, and Jenny bounces from foot to foot while rubbing a hand over her back.

"How you settling in?"

Jenny's one of the sweetest people I've ever met. She's co-owner of Beautiful Blossoms, although not for much longer. Jenny's selling her half of the business to start a flower farm up in the mountains. It sounds idyllic.

"I'm loving it," I say truthfully. "It's nice meeting so many different people."

She has no idea how much of an understatement that is.

My family only associated with other rich families. The kids I grew up with were all entitled, rich, and boring, believing the world owed them something.

I love the customer interaction I get working at Beautiful Blossoms. This small town is miles away from the coastal rich playground I grew up in.

Jenny gives me a wide smile. "Good. I'm glad you like it here. We're lucky to have found you."

Beautiful Blossoms is the first proper job I've ever had. Sure, I helped Dad out with his business. I learned how to do accounts, talk with suppliers, and negotiate deals, but I've never done front-facing customer service before, and I've definitely never worked somewhere where they didn't know who I was or didn't give me special treatment because I was the boss's daughter.

I learned a lot about business from my dad, but not like this.

Aria comes out from the back of the shop. "I thought I heard you," she exclaims when she sees Jenny. Her eyes immediately go to the sleeping baby. "How is she today?"

"She's fine. Due to wake up again soon."

Aria's own belly protrudes with a pregnancy bump, and she rubs it absentmindedly.

"Do you mind if we get some lunch?" Aria asks me.

I've only been here two weeks, and they already trust me to be alone in the shop. I don't know if that's a credit to how well my dad taught me or if everyone's this trusting in a small town. It's a far cry from the business world my father operates in where you constantly have to watch your back.

I like the trust that's here.

And I like these two women, who have started up this business and have this cool friendship together. I feel wistful thinking about my sister, Chastity, who's also my closest friend. Or was, until I ran away.

"I'll be fine," I say, brushing aside thoughts of Chastity before they overwhelm me.

"We'll be at Candy's Café if you need us."

Aria grabs her coat and slides it on. The two women head out, and the shop bell jingles after them.

I lean my elbows on the counter and watch them walk down the street together, laughing and chatting.

Maple Springs may only be a few hundred miles up the coast from Cod Cove, but it feels like a million miles away.

I just hope my father can't find me here.

There's a stab of guilt when I think about my father and leaving the way I did. But I had to get away from him, away from his influence and control.

I just hope he understands why I had to leave. I need some space, some independence to do things on my own, and the only way to do that was by leaving.

I'll get in touch with Mom soon so she knows I'm safe. But I also know Dad will track any communication and do anything to get me back. And I'm not ready to go back yet.

He'll be furious that I've left, and there's no knowing what my father will do when he's angry. Thinking about my dad makes me shudder, and I reach for my purse.

My hand grips the Smith & Wesson, and the cold metal feels reassuring. I take a few deep breaths before releasing the gun into my handbag.

2
KARL

The table I've chosen is in the far corner of the cafe, pressed against the wall and half obscured by the coffee machine. With my laptop open and cap pulled low, I look like just any other guy working in the cafe.

But the notes I'm typing are only about one thing: Trinity.

It took me almost three weeks to find her.

The few friends she had in Cod Cove were all surprised she'd run away. They thought she enjoyed working for her dad. They thought she'd take over the family business one day.

The picture they painted of a smart, serious young woman is miles away from the spoiled brat I initially pegged her as.

It became clear Trinity wasn't on a yacht somewhere like I first thought. And if there's a man involved, then none of her friends know about it.

I tracked all the buses that passed through the Sunset

Coast the day she left. A driver thought he remembered someone who fit her description and got off in Portland.

Using my contacts, I pulled the CCTV footage from the station and saw her board another bus heading inland to Boise. But she never made it to Boise.

I checked every stop along the route, pulling CCTV footage where they had it and doing a tour of the towns that didn't.

Then one day, there she was, crossing the street in front of my car, her dark hair streaming down her back, a slight smile on her face as she sipped her coffee.

She didn't see me. But I watched her.

For the last three days, I've watched her, making notes on where she goes, who she speaks to, and what she likes. Getting to know her before I make my move.

I've got it all on file on my laptop.

Trinity works at Beautiful Blossoms, a flower shop owned by two women who trust her enough to leave her alone in the shop.

I know she brings her own lunch to work, which she eats on a bench under a maple tree in the park, and she always feeds the pigeons some crumbs.

I know she goes to Candy's Café for her afternoon break and comes out with a takeaway cup and a smile on her face.

Yesterday I followed her after work when she walked down Main Street exploring the shops.

Then she went straight home to number thirty-two on Curzon Street, a row of cheap rental houses on the edge of town.

In the three days I've been watching Trinity, she hasn't

meet with anyone. Her main social contact seems to be in the cafe where she spends her fifteen-minute afternoon break.

Which is why I'm here today, waiting and watching for her. I want to know what she orders, what makes her smile, why it takes fifteen goddamn minutes to get a coffee.

My fingers drum my thigh under the table. If it's a man she's coming in here for, I'm going to lose it.

The protectiveness I feel over Trinity has only increased since I found her. She's mine, clear and simple, and I'll hurt anyone who gets between us.

The door to the cafe opens, and my breath hitches. It's her. Trinity.

I drink her in, my whole body on alert and my blood pounding in my ears at the sight of her.

She's wearing a tight black t-shirt that shows off the delicious curves of her breasts. She's carrying a bit of weight, which looks good on her, making her soft and feminine. Her womanly shape makes my dick twitch in my trousers.

She walks to the counter and greets the boy behind it by name. The smile she gives him lights up her whole face, and a pang of jealousy pierces my heart.

There's a growl deep in my chest. If she's fucking this kid, I'm going to rip his fucking head off.

"I'll have a chai latte with soy milk."

I don't know what the fuck a chai latte is, but it's just become my favorite drink.

"Sweet or spicy?" the kid asks.

"Spicy."

I make a note on my laptop, adding the drink to the list I'm making of things I know about Trinity.

She talks with the kid as he makes her coffee. He can't be long out of school with his baby face and dewy skin.

My fists clench under the table.

That's not what Trinity needs. She needs a man who can take care of her. A man like me.

While the boy's making the drink, a woman with blue hair in two bunches comes in from out back. She's carrying a baby on her hip and smiles warmly when she sees Trinity.

"Did you find Vulcan Lane?"

I do a quick internet search on Vulcan Lane. It's a plaza off Main Street known for its art and vintage shops.

I followed Trinity down there yesterday.

"I loved it! I found this cute little purse." She holds up a vintage beaded purse, and the woman coos over it like it's a baby.

The boy hands her the drink, and Trinity and the woman sit at a table talking animatedly. So, this is what she comes in for. It's not the kid. It's the female friend.

As they talk, Trinity takes the baby, bouncing it on her lap.

It suits her, having a baby on her knee. One day it'll be mine she's holding.

While the women talk, the kid comes out from behind the counter and takes a coffee to a table where a woman dressed in business attire is tapping away on her laptop.

She gives him a warm smile, and he plants a kiss on her lips.

My fists relax.

Somehow this babyface has bagged an older woman. She's got to be at least ten years older, and when she stands up, I notice a round baby bump. What is it about this place that everyone's got a kid or one on the way?

At least it's not the boy that Trinity's coming in here for. It's the blue-haired woman. Bella, I heard her call her. Just a bit of human company and friendship.

Trinity didn't run away to be with a man. As far as I can tell, she ran away to get out from under her family and away from the life of privilege where everyone is concerned with the latest fashion and diets and wouldn't be caught dead in a cozy small-town cafe like this one.

There's a peel of laughter from the table, and Trinity giggles at something Bella has said.

She seems happy here.

Trinity likes small-town life. She likes small-town people. And if that's what she wants, that's what I'll fucking be.

I'll buy a flannelette shirt and a pair of worn jeans. I'll go unshaven and wear a baseball cap permanently.

She likes small town, so I'll become small town. I'll become anything she needs me to be.

As Trinity leaves the cafe, my phone rings.

It's Damon.

"You find her yet?"

I watch Trinity through the window, noting the curves of her ass through her black leggings as she walks away.

"Afraid not, boss. Another dead end."

Damon grunts down the phone. "Her mother's distraught."

There's a pang of guilt for the mother, and for Damon, but if they'd treated Trinity better, maybe she would have stuck around. Trinity obviously doesn't want to be with her family, and I'll do whatever Trinity wants.

"I've got a lead," I lie. "She's further north."

"Okay."

"I'm heading to Seattle tomorrow." I keep talking, hoping Damon buys it. "I'll go up there and take a look. But it feels like she really doesn't want to be found."

"I'm counting on you, Karl. You find my girl and bring her back home."

I hang up the phone.

I'll bring her home, all right. Home to me.

3

TRINITY

I'm out back when the bell above the door jingles.

"Be with you in a minute," I call.

Selecting a couple of bunches of peonies, I carry them through to the shop and set them in one of the buckets by the counter.

The man has his back to me, crouching over a display of colorful blooms. He's big and broad-shouldered, and he looks out of place in the feminine flower shop.

My heart races. It's one of Dad's men come to fetch me home. Then the man stands up. He's wearing a worn flannelette shirt, faded jeans, and a well-thumbed baseball cap.

My body relaxes. It's another local, not one of my dad's men.

He's looking at the colorful display of pretty freesias and carnations in yellows and pinks. They're the kind of flowers you'd give a colleague, or a sister, or your mom.

The man turns around, and our eyes lock. His look is

intense, his gaze boring into mine with intensity. As if he knows me already. As if he knows everything about me and can see into my soul. There's a crackle of electricity in the air, and I take a step backward. My hand flies to my chest. I wonder if he felt it too.

Then his look softens, and he smiles slightly. Just another stranger. I wonder if I imagined it.

"I'm looking for flowers for my mom."

His voice is gravelly and deep, as intense as the look he just gave me. There's dark stubble around his chin, and I have an urge to run my palm over it, to feel the roughness chafe my skin.

He gives me a lopsided smile, and I drop my gaze quickly, suddenly certain he can read my thoughts.

"Is it a special occasion?"

"Her birthday." He turns back to the flowers. "I can't decide if I should go for pink or yellow."

He shrugs his big shoulders, and it touches me, this big burly man buying flowers for him mom.

"Yellow matches the season, and we've got these premade bouquets that come with foliage to complement the freesias."

I come out from behind the counter to show him the bouquets in the display at the back of the shop.

"Ah yes. Perfect."

The man comes right up close to me, and I catch a whiff of something spicy. A masculine cinnamon body wash.

My body quivers, and there's heat between my legs.

I step away quickly, scurrying back to the safety of the

counter. This stranger is having all sorts of effects on my body. It's disconcerting.

He places the bouquet on the counter, and I grab a sheet of cellophane.

"I'll just wrap this up for you."

His eyes watch my lips, and I feel nervous, my fingers fumbling under his gaze.

"I'm Karl."

"Trina."

"Trina," he repeats as if testing my name out on his tongue.

I probably should have come up with a different name when I ran away, but Trina is close enough to feel like my own, but different enough so as not to give me away.

"Nice shop you've got here." He's talking about the shop, but his gaze remains on me.

"I don't own it. I just work here."

I tie up the flowers, but my hands are restless under his gaze. I put a sprinkling of chocolate hearts in the wrapping.

"Can you send these for me?"

"Sure." I show him the price list, and he writes an address for me.

"You want to write a note?"

I hand him one of our cards, and I wait while he writes. I try not to look, but I'm too nosy.

Dear Ma,

Happy Birthday. Enjoy your night out with the bingo ladies.

Love, Karl

My heart softens. A man who sends his mother

flowers on her birthday has to be a good guy. I also note the lack of a ring on his finger.

Karl takes his wallet out, and I look away quickly but not before I see how thick it is with cash. He puts a hundred-dollar bill on the counter, and I count out the change.

"I'm new to town. You know any decent cafes?"

"I'm new too."

It slips out before I realize what I've said.

Way to play it cool, Trinity. If I'm going to stay hidden from my family, I shouldn't advertise the fact that I'm the new girl in town.

But Karl just smiles. "It seems like a nice place."

"Candy's Café is good. The staff are friendly."

"Candy's Café..." Karl tilts his head.

I suddenly have this weird feeling that he's going to ask me out. Which is crazy since I just met the guy.

"I think I passed that on Main Street. Thanks, Trina. Have a good day."

He turns away, and I let out a breath I didn't know I was holding.

As I watch him leave the shop, a pang of disappointment goes through me, which is stupid. Why would a complete stranger ask me out?

4

KARL

The moving truck backs into the driveway about a half hour before Trinity is due home. If I've timed it right, she'll be pulling up just about when my furniture will be moving in.

Not that it's my furniture. I bought it all new and held it at a storage unit until I could arrange this charade. The tenants needed a little convincing to vacate the premises, but it wasn't anything that a cash incentive couldn't fix.

I'm helping the moving guys pull a couch out of the truck when Trinity's car pulls up next door. It takes all my restraint not to stare at her, to play it cool. But my blood's thundering in my ears just knowing that she's close by.

It's not until the car door slams that I allow myself to look up. Our eyes lock across the driveway, and I mirror her look of surprise.

"Hey, Tina."

"Trina," she corrects me.

I look apologetic for my supposed gaff as I make my way across the strip of lawn that separates our houses.

"From the florist shop, right?" As if I don't know. As if I don't know every goddamn thing about her.

"That's right. You came in to buy flowers for your mom. Karl, isn't it?"

It's been two days since our encounter at the florist, and the fact she remembers me sends warmth through my bones. A kernel of hope unfurls in my stomach.

"You moving in?" she asks.

I glance at the moving van parked outside and the two men carrying a couch.

"What gave it away?"

She laughs, and it's good to see how carefree she looks. She's happy here. There's no way I could ever betray her and take her back to her family.

"Welcome to the neighborhood." She opens her arms expansively.

"You live around here?" I let the surprise creep into my voice.

"Right next door."

I raise my eyebrows in surprise. "No way."

She laughs again. "Gotta love a small town."

We chat for a bit as she tells me about the neighbors. I watch the movement of her lips, the way her tongue pokes out when she laughs, the tiny lines at the corners of her mouth.

After watching Trinity from afar, it's tantalizing having her so close. It takes all my restraint not to reach out for her, to run my fingers over her cheek, to tangle them in her hair.

I stuff my hands in my pockets to keep from touching

her. It's too soon to make my move. I'm playing for keeps, and that means waiting.

One of the moving men asks me a question, and I give Trinity an apologetic look.

"I gotta go. I need to tell these guys where to put everything."

"Of course." She waves me away. "It was nice to see you again."

I turn and leave, letting her watch me go. I'm playing the long game here, and I can be patient.

My phone lights up the dark room, and I lunge for it, knowing already who it will be.

"Damon."

"What's going on up there, Karl?"

There's an edge to his voice. He's getting agitated and probably getting pressure from his wife. I need to give him something.

"Some good news."

"You found her?"

The hope in his voice makes me waver. I feel a pang of guilt for the father who wants his daughter back. But then I think of Trinity smiling and content here, and my self-ishness takes over. I want her to myself.

"Not exactly. She was here, though. I believe she's crossed the border."

"To Canada?"

"Afraid so. I'm gonna head up there and take a look. Might be gone a while."

"Do what you need to do. I'm looking after things here."

"All right, boss."

I hang up the phone and resume my position by the window.

Through the binoculars, I can see straight into Trinity's room. She hasn't pulled the curtains yet, and I watch her paint her toenails. She must be bored. In a new town and with no friends, Trinity must be desperate for some company, ready to make a new friend or take a lover.

It's just the right time to make my move, to be the companion she needs.

She's sitting on the bed, leaning over her feet, and her top has fallen open, revealing the soft flesh of the top of her breasts.

My cock hardens watching her. Her tits are pushed together. They're just the right size to slide my cock between.

My dick lengthens, straining against my jeans. With one hand holding the binoculars, I ease my dick out with the other.

Stroking my length, I watch Trinity as she sets the bottle of nail varnish down on the bedside table. She leans back on her elbows, giving me a good look at her body. Even fully clothed she's got me panting, worked up enough to tug at my cock while I imagine all the things I'd like to do to her.

I bet she smells fucking good, like rose petals and pussy. I'd love to bury myself between her legs and make her scream my name as I suck her cunt.

My balls pull up tight, and I move the binoculars so I can see her mouth. Those plump lips wrapped around my cock. That's what I think about as I jerk myself off, imagining fucking Trinity's mouth, her pussy, her ass, every hole, everywhere she can take me. I want to claim her, destroy her, watch her scream my name as I make her mine.

I come in an explosion of heat and sweat, my cum shooting out of my dick to coat the windowpane.

I'm breathing hard as I smear it over the cool glass, blurring my view of her. But I'm not satisfied. I won't be satisfied until I have the real thing.

5

TRINITY

Candy's Café smells like cinnamon and coffee when I step inside a few days later. There's a small line ahead of me, and I tap my feet impatiently. I've only got fifteen minutes for my break, and I need my fix.

I'm looking at my phone, so I don't notice the man at the front of the line until I hear his voice.

"I'll have a spicy chai latte with soy milk."

I'd recognize that deep voice anywhere. Karl, my new neighbor, and he's got the exact same taste in hot drinks as me.

The universe is practically throwing this man in front of me.

First, that intense meeting at the florist. Then he moves in next door. And now here he is ordering the same drink I like. That must mean something.

"Karl?"

He turns around, and his eyes go wide when he sees me.

"Hey, Trina. Can I get you something?"

His smile is wide and genuine with none of the intensity of our first meeting. Just a friendly neighbor offering me a drink.

Disappointment creeps into the pit of my stomach.

"Sure. Same as you."

He raises his eyebrows in surprise. "You like chai lattes?"

"With soy milk and cinnamon."

Karl chuckles. "And I thought I was the only weirdo."

He buys the drinks and ushers me over to a seat.

"I don't have long. I have to get back to the florist soon."

But I pull out the chair, wanting to sit with him, wanting to spend time with this man.

"How are you settling into the new place?"

"I've got my internet hooked up, so I'm fine."

When he smiles there're tiny lines around his eyes that never really go away. I'm guessing Karl's around thirty-something, probably ten years older than me. I've always felt comfortable with older men, thanks to working with my dad, so his age doesn't bother me.

"What brought you to Maple Springs?"

Karl takes a sip of his drink, leaving a line of froth over his top lip. I wonder what he'd do if I leaned over and licked it off.

His tongue flicks out and sucks the froth off his upper lip. My gaze watches his tongue. The quick movement sends a quiver between my thighs, and I clasp them together under the table, wondering what his tongue would feel like between my legs.

"Are you okay?"

I realize I'm staring, and I've got no idea what he's just said. A blush creeps up my cheeks. I duck my head so he can't see.

"Yeah. I better get back to work."

"You sure you're okay?"

Karl's hand reaches out and rests on my forearm. It's a light reassuring touch, but the contact sends sparks coursing through my body. His hand sears my skin where it rests.

My gaze flicks to his, and for a moment, I see the intensity from our first meeting, the unseen connection pulling us together.

I've never been with a man before. Sure, I've tumbled around with some of the local boys, but they were always so big-headed and full of expectations that I never found any I wanted to go all the way with.

Karl is different. I know in that single touch that he'd know what to do with my body, that he'd know where to put his hands and his quick-moving tongue.

My pussy trembles just thinking about it, and there's a rush of dampness between my legs.

"Do you want to come over for dinner one night?"

I blurt the words out while I'm feeling bold, before I can change my mind.

I left Cod Cove because I wanted a different life, but it's a lonely life. I'm tired of spending my nights alone at home. Why shouldn't I ask my hot new neighbor over for dinner?

Karl's smile softens. "Sure, I'd love that. How's tomorrow night?"

"Um, let me check my schedule." I pretend to check my

phone, but I already know I'm not doing anything. Not tonight, not tomorrow, not ever. I never knew how lonely it would be starting in a new town.

"Come by about seven."

It's only when I move that he takes his hand away from my arm.

The whole way back to the florist, I can feel the pressure of his touch and the heat he left behind on my skin.

6

KARL

I wait until ten minutes past seven before I knock on Trinity's door.

"Sorry I'm late. Had a client I had to deal with."

I hand her a bottle of red wine, which pairs perfectly with the lamb cutlets she's making. I know because I watched her flick through a recipe book last night.

Her house is small, like mine. A simple two-bedroom made for a single person or small family. She's renting, like I am, only hers is furnished with an odd array of items she must have picked up from the local charity shop.

"Sorry about the mismatched furniture," she says, sweeping her hand over the wooden table with mismatched chairs. "But I think it has a certain charm."

She doesn't look at all concerned that a few weeks ago she was living in luxury and now she's in a drafty rental with secondhand furniture and faded wallpaper.

But Trinity doesn't seem to mind. She looks at home

in this humble lodging, wearing an apron and humming to herself as she pulls a roasting tray out of the oven.

When she's mine, Trinity can have any furniture she wants. If she wants to decorate the house in reclaimed second-hand couches, she can do that. If she wants plush carpets and designer furniture, she can have that too.

I've been clever with my money over the years and invested it well. Trinity won't want for anything.

She sets the plates, and we sit facing each other across the table.

I bite into a roasted potato, and it splinters in my mouth. I try not to cringe at the burnt taste.

Trinity's watching me anxiously, and I force myself to chew the food she's spent so long preparing.

"It's awful, isn't it?"

She's wide-eyed and anxious, but I can't lie. The potatoes are burnt and the meat is so dry it's more like jerky.

"It's, um…" I swallow the potato, and it gets lodged in my throat, making me cough. I take a large swig of wine to wash it down.

"Are you okay?"

I thump my chest, feeling the lump of potato making its way slowly down my esophagus.

"Yeah." My eyes are watering, and I'm trying not to laugh. "I take it you don't cook much?"

"Never." She looks miserable. "I never learned how to cook."

This isn't news to me. I've learned all about Trinity's life from before she became Trina. The Fletchers have a team of domestic employees—a housekeeper, a butler, a cook, a gardener, and even a nanny until Trinity was fourteen.

But I don't let Trinity know this. I tilt my head and wait for her to speak, wondering how much she's going to tell me.

"I grew up quite privileged."

"Really?"

It's hard, keeping up this pretense that I don't know anything about her. But if I'm going to win Trinity over, this has to feel authentic.

"I only came to Maple Springs about four weeks ago."

"You're new, like me."

She looks down at her food, pushing the dried meat around the plate.

"Do you have family here?"

I'm pushing her now, seeing how far she'll go, what she'll tell me and how much she'll lie. It feels like a test, but I'm not exactly sure what I'm testing her for.

"Not around here."

She stands up from the table quickly. "You wanna get takeout?"

"Sure."

She looks relieved, and I'm not sure if it's because she dodged the questions about her family or if she's relieved about the food.

While Trinity goes off to hunt for a menu, I take the plates to the kitchen.

I feel relieved too. She didn't lie to me, and I like that. A relationship shouldn't be built on lies, which I know is hypocritical of me.

We order pizza and eat it sitting on her two-seater couch while drinking the wine.

"What is it you do?"

Trinity hasn't asked me much about why I came here, and I expect it's because she doesn't want to answer the same questions about herself.

"I work in IT."

I've rehearsed this so many times. I tell her about my fake consulting business. It's easy to fudge the details. That's why I chose IT. Throw in a few technical phrases and most people won't question what you tell them.

"I mostly work from home, so I can work from anywhere."

"And you chose here. Why?"

Her feet are tucked up under her, and her empty wine glass sits on the table next to greasy pizza boxes.

I want to tell her it was her. She's the reason why I'm here. Because once I saw her photo, there was no going back. There was no other place for me but by her side.

But I can't tell her that.

"It seems like a nice quiet town."

Trinity nods like she knows what I mean. "I like it here too."

A strand of hair falls over her cheek, and I twist it in my fingers before tucking it behind her ear. Her eyes dart to mine, and her lips part slightly.

My heart rate climbs a notch. She's prettier than her photo, prettier than anything I've ever seen. My hand moves to her cheek, stroking the soft skin. I trail my finger over her lips, pulling her plump lips apart.

Trinity whimpers and shuffles forward in her seat.

She's coming to me, and I let her come. I wait until she leans forward, her eyes closed and lips parted. I know it's her choice. However we got to this point, she's making the first move.

Then my lips are on hers, claiming her mouth. She tastes like peperoni and merlot, the grease on her lips making our mouths slip.

My hand goes behind her head and tangles in her hair, pulling her toward me. I've waited so long for this moment. I've imagined it, dreamt about it. She's filled my thoughts, made me go out of my mind.

My lips move down her neck, running over her skin, tasting her soft flesh, licking and nibbling at her throat.

"Karl…"

Her breathy voice makes me pause and come up for air. If she's unsure, I'll back off. I'll bide my time until she's ready. But when I see her eyes, hooded with desire, my dick hardens and I know she's as into this as I am.

"Come upstairs."

She stands up and offers me her hand. With my heart thumping and my cock stiff, I follow Trinity to her bedroom.

7

TRINITY

My palms are sweaty, my pulse racing as I lead Karl upstairs. I've never done anything like this before. I want to go through with it before I change my mind.

We get to my bedroom, and I hesitate on the threshold. I felt bold downstairs, but now I feel shy.

"You okay, sweetheart?"

Karl cups my face, and his kiss sends volts of energy through my body. I melt in his hands, and I know without a doubt that I want this man.

I may have led him upstairs, but now Karl takes control. He lifts me up and, with our lips still pressed together, carries me over to the bed.

He pushes me gently backward, and I fall onto the soft covers as he hovers above me.

"I've wanted this for so long," Karl murmurs as he kisses my neck.

It doesn't make sense because we only met a few days ago, but nothing about how I feel about him makes sense.

We shed our clothes until our bodies press together, his rough stubble grating against my smooth skin as he explores me with his mouth, nuzzling and nibbling my most sensitive areas.

His hands are all over my breasts, pulling and squeezing until my nipples ache with longing. They pebble hard as he takes one into his mouth, and I moan at the sensation. It feels like my whole body is on fire, heat from my nipples winding all the way to my core.

His hands run over my thighs and between my legs.

I gasp, sitting up on my elbows, and Karl's gaze meets mine. His look is hungry. It makes my pussy throb with need.

"I've never done this before, Karl."

I bite my lower lip, suddenly nervous. I barely know this man, yet I'm ready to give my virginity to him.

"You're a virgin?" His voice comes out ragged, like he can barely hold himself back.

"Yeah." I hold my breath, not sure if he'll want to carry on.

"Oh, sweetheart." Karl kisses me softly on my breast, moving his way back up my body so he's at eye level with me on the bed.

"I promise I'll look after you, Trina." He kisses my forehead, and I don't know if he means in the bedroom or in life. "I'll always look after you."

Whichever it is, I feel safe with him. I believe him.

His lips move to the corners of my mouth and leave soft, teasing kisses. "But your first time will hurt. I can't help that."

My pussy clenches and nervousness creeps into my

belly. Karl keeps kissing me softly, slowly making his way back down my body.

"I don't want it to hurt," I whisper.

"But you do want me to fuck you?"

Karl's tongue flicks out at my nipple, a quick, hot, wet sensation that makes me shudder. It feels as good as I imagined his tongue would feel.

"Yes," I gasp.

"I need you to use your words, sweetheart." I stare at him and my belly clenches. I'm not sure what I'm meant to do here.

His tongue flicks the other nipple, and I whimper.

I'm terrified he'll think I'm too inexperienced and stop what he's doing with his wicked tongue.

"Tell me what you want me to do to you."

His gaze meets mine as his hand slides over my engorged pussy. "Tell me, Trina."

"I want…" It's hard to say the words. Sure, I've said fuck a thousand times, but not in this context, not with a hard man on top of me ready to do wicked things to my body.

"I want you to…"

His thumb finds my sensitive nub, and my words turn to a moan as he circles my clit.

"Say it."

Karl's voice is commanding, and it reverberates through me.

"I want you to fuck me."

As I say it, his finger slides into my pussy and my words come out as a gasp. My head tilts back, and I open my thighs, wanting more of what he's giving me.

"Good girl."

Said in his gravelly voice, the praise makes me whimper. I want to please Karl. I want him to tell me what to do. And most of all, I want him to keep doing what he's doing.

My hands clasp the duvet cover as his head ducks between my thighs. When his mouth closes over my pussy, I just about lose it. It's like nothing I've ever felt before. The heat, the wetness, his stubble scaping against my thighs.

I grab the duvet cover as my ass lifts off the bed, my body writhing in protest at the vulnerability and the sweet sensation coming together to form one confusing ball of sensations.

He kisses me slowly, and I begin to relax. The licking, nibbling, and circling fall into a rhythm, and my body responds.

Until I can't take it anymore. Grabbing Karl's hair, I pull him toward me, deeper between my legs. Needing more friction, needing a release, needing everything he's got. My pussy rubs shamelessly against his face as I moan Karl's name.

My body releases, exploding over his face and sending shock waves coursing through my body. I scream his name as I grip his hair, pushing myself against him until the vibrations become something I can stand.

I'm panting as he lifts his head and moves on top of me.

"Good girl. Now I want you to do that again, and again, and again."

His hands press on my thighs, and he guides his dick

toward my opening. I'm nervous about my first time, but I also feel loose—relaxed and ready for him.

Karl's dick slides into me, and there's a red-hot pain. My eyes squeeze shut, and I cry out. Karl pauses, half inside me.

"Take a big breath and open your eyes, sweetheart."

I do as he says and feel my body relax.

"You okay?"

There's need in his eyes and also concern. I know if I asked him to stop now, he would. But I don't want him to stop. I want to push through the pain to the pleasure that I know will be on the other side.

"Keep going, Karl. I want you to fuck me."

He groans at my dirty words, and seeing his pleasure makes my nipples pebble. Knowing I have this power over him makes me bold. I look him dead in the eye.

"Fuck my virgin pussy, Karl."

Karl swallows hard. His neck pulses with need and restraint.

"Only when you're ready." His voice is clipped, his jaw set as he struggles to restrain himself.

"Do it, Karl. Fuck me now."

I feel satisfaction as I watch the moment he loses control.

His cock slams into me, and I cry out at the sharp pain. But even as it burns, I wrap my legs around him, embracing the pain and moving with him until the sensation turns to rumblings of delicious pleasure.

"Fuuck," I moan, enjoying the new sensation, the fullness I feel.

"That's it, sweetheart. The worst is over. Now I'm going to make you enjoy it."

He moves slowly, and my pussy relaxes. More than relaxes. The sensation builds, like a wonderful pressure.

I grab hold of Karl's shoulders and dig my nails into his skin as the orgasm rips through me, the pleasure so overwhelming that I leave deep claw marks on his back.

"Good girl," Karl says each time I come.

After each release, he builds me up again until I explode on the end of his cock, my body writhing uncontrollably.

Until I feel broken like a rag doll with no bones in my body.

Only then does Karl let himself go. He thrusts into me, slamming hard until I feel his balls bouncing up against my back passage, sending a whole new set of sensations through my body.

Just when I think I've got nothing left in me, I come once more, and as I do, he joins me, his cum shooting inside me in hot, sticky strips.

Karl's body tenses as he comes, and he pulls me close until I think he'll crush me in his arms.

When he releases me, I fall onto the bed exhausted.

Karl tucks me in and plants soft kisses on my cheek. I'm so tired I can't keep my eyes open.

As I drift off to sleep, I must start dreaming because I imagine that I hear Karl whisper, "I love you."

8

KARL

Two weeks later…

"What do you mean she's gone to Europe?"

The fury in Damon's voice makes me wince. I hold the phone away from my ear as he curses, letting his anger out down the phone.

"She's gone traveling, backpacking."

"Backpacking," Damon snorts. "Last time we were in Europe, we stayed on a super yacht in Biarritz. No daughter of mine needs to backpack."

I give him time to rant, knowing I need to handle this delicately.

I need Damon to halt his search for Trinity for a while. I need him to believe she's off seeing the world and will come back when she's ready.

He'd kill me now if he knew I was fucking his daughter. But once we're married and I've put a baby in her belly, he'll have no choice but to accept it.

It's better to ask forgiveness than permission.

"She just needs space. I'm sure she'll come back when she's seen a bit of the world."

"Are you telling me what my daughter needs?"

I think back to last night, to Trinity on her knees, her pleading eyes looking at me over her shoulder as she begged me to put my cock in her.

"I need you to fuck me," she pleaded.

Yeah, I know what Damon's daughter needs, but I'm not stupid enough to tell him that.

"No, sir," I say.

There's silence on the other end of the phone, and I hear a glass clinking.

"You want me to follow her to Europe? Because I really think she'll come back after she's…"

"No," Damon snaps, cutting me off. "I want you to come back here. You were tasked with finding my daughter, and you failed."

I take a deep breath.

It's not good to piss the boss off, but he's playing right into my hands.

I want out. I'm done with Fletcher Holdings. I've bought into my own fantasy right here in Maple Springs.

I want a quiet life, a low-profile job. It doesn't matter where that is or what I do, as long as I'm with Trinity.

Once we're married, we'll come back and make peace with her family. Then we'll go somewhere far away from them, somewhere quiet, just the two of us.

But first I need to make a clean break with Damon. He's not the type of man you want loose ends with.

"I'll wrap things up here and be back in a few days."

. . .

Twenty minutes after Trinity gets home, I knock on her front door and enter without waiting for an answer. I've been in and out of her house so much over the last two weeks that I'm practically living here.

Trinity's in the kitchen washing dishes, and she smiles when she sees me.

"You finished for the day?"

"Yeah," I lie. "Just wrapped up with my last client."

The truth is I spend my days waiting for Trinity to get home.

We've spent every night for the last two weeks together. Always in her bed where the worn duvet cover makes it feel like a home. We wake up together, make love, and get ready like a regular couple.

She goes off to work, and I pretend to go to my house as if I've got a line of clients waiting for me on the other side of a computer screen.

But once she's left the house, I follow her, keeping a safe distance so she never sees me. I watch her go into Beautiful Blossoms, and I make a note of every customer who goes in there.

I'm racked with jealousy every time another man goes into the florist, ready to run in and beat him to the ground if he lays one finger on her.

Sometimes I call to see if she wants to meet for lunch, pretending that I'm calling from home and not from across the street.

We meet at Candy's and drink spiced chai lattes, which I've come to tolerate. She tells me about her customers, and I make up stories about annoying clients.

In the evening, I pretend I'm still working when she

gets home, then I come around and we eat and talk and fuck.

It's pure heaven, a beautiful love story. Our time together is sweet and special and fun. Others would envy our connection, the comfortable way we are together, and the explosive sex we have as we explore each other's bodies. Trinity goes off like a firecracker every time I get close to her sensitive nub.

Yet, as each day goes by, an anxiousness gnaws at me. There's an uneasy feeling in my gut that this charmed existence can't last. That Trinity will find out about me, or she'll want to go back to her old life.

The anxiety makes me possessive, makes the need in me grow until I can't rest until I have her. I have to possess her. I have to make sure she's real, that all of this is real.

Her hands are in the sink, and I come up behind her, sliding my hands around her waist and straight down to her pussy.

"Hey, I'm doing chores," she teases.

"Not anymore."

My body presses into her back, bumping her against the sink so she can feel my hard cock. My hand slides into the sink and over hers, stroking her wrists.

"Did you have a good day?"

"Better now."

I should be gentle. I should chitchat and make up stories about my day. But there's no gentleness inside me today, just a need to make sure Trinity is mine.

My mouth is rough on her neck, sweeping away the hair and biting at her skin, making her gasp.

My hand comes out of the sink, and I slide it over her breast.

"Hey, you're making my top wet."

"Good."

She spins around all indignant and flicks me with dishwater.

I grab her wrists, and she squeals as I pull her against me. The water has made her white top stick to her bra, and I can see the lacy fabric underneath.

I hoist her wrists up over her head, and she squirms against me, trying to get out of my grasp. But the movements only make my cock harder and my need stronger.

"You're not going anywhere, little girl."

Trinity takes a sharp intake of breath and her lips part, her eyes hooded with desire.

Hey!" Trinity protests, and I cover her mouth with mine. Her protests turn to moans as I kiss her hard.

With one hand still holding her wrists, I use the other to shimmy her away from the sink and hoist her onto the kitchen counter.

I let her wrists go, and she wraps her hands in my hair, pulling me toward her. I love it when she wears a skirt. I part her thighs and roughly run my hand over her dripping panties. I can't be gentle today. I need her too badly.

Her panties are wet, and I pull them aside, not bothering to take them off.

Her hands are on my belt, pulling it open with the same urgency that I feel. A few seconds later, I thrust my dick deep inside her, burying myself in her sweet, warm haven. Her sweet pussy tugs at my length as I fuck her on the kitchen counter.

Her legs go around my waist, and I slide a hand under her hips so I can slam deeper into her tight cunt.

"Karl…" She pants my name as I thrust into her.

"You're mine." I slam into her hungry pussy.

"Mine, mine, mine."

I howl the word with every thrust, holding her head so she looks me in the eyes as I fuck her hard, until she's screaming my name as she comes.

Then I let myself go, shooting my hot semen into her and coating her womb.

I want to breed her. I want my seed to grow in her. I want to tie Trinity to me forever.

With my cock still in her, I take her chin and tilt her head so she's looking at me.

"I love you, Trina."

"I love you too, Karl."

It's the first time she's said it back to me, and my heart might explode alongside my cock. This is happiness. This is what it feels like.

"I want to do right by you, Trina. I want to marry you. I want to start a life together. You and me, somewhere new."

Her eyes glisten, and she looks down.

"I have to tell you something."

She bites her lower lip, and I love how anxious she is. She doesn't know that I already know all about her. Nothing she could say would surprise me.

"I need to tell you about my family."

I feign surprise. "What is it, sweetheart?"

I'm still nestled between her legs, my cum sticky on

her thighs. It's the sweetest place in the whole fucking world.

"You asked me once why I came to Maple Springs." It's hard for her to say, and I want to tell her it's okay, that I already know, but I've got to let her speak.

"I ran away from my family."

I nod my head slowly, letting it come out in her own words.

"My father is a rich man, a powerful man. He had expectations for me, a life mapped out working for him. But he's not always legit. Some of the things he does…"

She looks up at me anxiously as if this could change how I feel about her.

"Go on, sweetheart."

Her brow's furrowed, showing the internal struggle she's going through telling me this, and my heart goes out to her.

"I came to Maple Springs because I wanted independence. I wanted to see if I could make it on my own."

"Do they know where you are?"

"No. My dad's controlling. If he knew where I was, he'd send one of his thugs to come and get me."

She knows her old man so well. I'm that thug. A pang of guilt pierces my chest. I feel like a prime asshole as Trinity pours her heart out to me.

She doesn't tell me her name or exactly who her family is, but it's as much of a confession as she's gonna give me.

When she's done, I put my arms around her. "Thank you for telling me."

She pulls back to look into my eyes. They're earnest. Honest.

"I don't want there to be any secrets between us, Karl."

Her eyes search mine, and I pray she doesn't see the lie sitting in them.

"No secrets."

As I hold her in my arms, I feel like the biggest asshole. No secrets, I said, but my whole existence in her life is a secret.

I need to sever my ties with her father and take Trinity far, far away from here.

9

TRINITY

'm humming to myself as I arrange the flower display at the front of the shop. I raise the dahlias to my nose and breathe deeply, closing my eyes and letting the sweet scent fill my nostrils.

Everything seems vivid today, the colors, the scents. I never noticed how many shades of purple there are in dahlias.

"You seem happy."

Aria smiles knowingly as she hands me a bucket of freesias to add to the display.

"Is it that new man you're seeing?"

My cheeks flush at mention of Karl, and I can't keep the grin off my face. The last two weeks together have been the happiest of my life.

I've never felt so free, so alive.

Karl and I just click, like we're meant to be together. We talk and we laugh and the sex is unbelievable. The things he can do to my body, the way he makes it hum—I never knew you could feel that good.

"Karl."

Even saying his name makes my insides quiver, and I can't hide the smile from my face.

Aria grins at me.

"You got it bad, girl." She leans in conspiratorially. "What's he like in bed?"

"I'm not telling you that."

"So, you are sleeping with him!" she says triumphantly, and I laugh at the way she caught me.

I hold my hands up. "Guilty."

The shop bell jingles, and Jenny comes in bouncing her baby on her hip.

"What are you two laughing about?"

A flush creeps up my neck, and I stifle a giggle.

"Trina's telling me about her boyfriend."

I've only known these women for a few weeks, but they've been so kind to me. I feel guilty that they don't know who I really am or my real name.

Jenny raises her eyebrows. "That big guy who's always hanging around waiting for you?"

He's been in the shop twice to visit. I wouldn't call that hanging around. She must mean someone else.

"Karl, with the checkered shirts and baseball cap."

Jenny nods. "Yeah, always sitting in his pickup across the road. Figured he must wait to take his break with you."

I frown at Jenny, but she seems convinced. Maybe she's got baby brain or something. She's not in the shop much at the moment, so she must be thinking of someone else.

"So, what does he do?" Aria asks.

"He's an IT consultant. Works from home mostly for remote clients."

"Where's he from? What's his family like? You don't know a man until you know about his family," Jenny says sagely, and I wonder what the history is with her man. I heard he's ex-military, a mountain recluse.

"Karl's mom lives in Reno."

I realize I only know that from the address he sent the flowers to. Karl doesn't talk about his family much. In fact, he doesn't talk about his past much at all.

Jenny and Aria are looking at me expectantly, like I should have more information, making me wonder if it's weird that I don't know much about Karl.

I told him my history last night, but what do I really know about him?

The door opens and a customer comes in. I jump to my feet, feeling relieved to end the conversation and trying to ignore the unsettled feeling in my gut.

A few hours later, I pull up outside my place. I finished early today, pretending to have a headache. Since my conversation with the girls this morning, I've felt uneasy.

I'm sure it's nothing. I'm sure if I just ask Karl about his past and about his family that he'll tell me.

Instead of going to my place, I cross the strip of grass that separates our houses and knock on his door.

There's no answer, and I wait a few moments before trying again.

Karl gave me a key in case I ever needed it, and I put it in the lock now and push open the door.

We've spent the last two weeks at my place, and I've never been inside his. He told me mine was cozier, that his was sparse and less homely. He wasn't lying.

There's nothing in the entryway aside from one pair of polished shoes.

"Hello," I call. But there's no answer. "Karl?"

He must be out visiting a client or running some errands. I should shut the door and go home, but I've never been inside his place and I'm curious.

At the end of the entryway, a door leads to the living room, and I wander through. The couch is a soft gray, the cushions plump and unwrinkled like they've barely been sat on.

I run my hand over the pristine fabric. There's a new smell about it, like it's just come from the furniture factory.

There's a glass coffee table with nothing on it, not even a scratch. Shelves built into the wall above the couch are empty.

I turn around slowly, taking in the space.

Karl wasn't lying when he said it was sparse. The place looks like a display in a furniture shop.

There are no photos, no plants, no ornaments. Only a couch, an armchair, and a coffee table.

The kernel of unease in my stomach grows into a stab of doubt.

I move through to the small dining area that leads to the kitchen.

There's an alcove with a dining table and four chairs in it. The table has a glass top, perfectly preserved like it's just had its protective plastic removed.

On the table sits a laptop. This must be where Karl works.

With my heart hammering in my chest, I take a seat and open the laptop.

I shouldn't look. I should back away. It's not cool to go snooping through your boyfriend's stuff. But I can't shake this uneasy feeling that something isn't right.

The laptop whirs to life, and I hold my breath. It's asking for a password, and I feel a strange sense of relief. I couldn't snoop even if I wanted to.

And what would be the point? It's just his work laptop. But there're no scribbled notes, no schedule, no papers scattered about his desk. It doesn't look like a place where someone works.

Positioning my fingers on the laptop, I take a deep breath. I'll just try a few words and see what happens.

Karl

Incorrect.

MapleSprings

Incorrect.

I bite my lower lip. I have no idea what a man like Karl would use as a password. This is pointless. I'm never going to get in.

Just for fun, I type:

Trinity

The laptop springs to life, and a bunch of files appear on the screen.

WTF?

I sit back, too surprised to process what's happened. Why the hell does he have Trinity as his password? It must be some weird coincidence.

A movement outside the window catches my eye.

Karl's pickup is pulling into the driveway.

"Shit."

Slamming the laptop closed, I spring out of his chair. I get to the door just as Karl comes in.

"Hey."

I make my voice steady even though my heart is racing.

"I finished early. Thought I'd stop by."

An anxious look crosses his face, and his eyes dart behind me into the house. I make my voice playful.

"I'm curious to see your place. Maybe you can give me a tour?" I plant a kiss on his lips, willing my heart to stop racing.

Karl relaxes and slides a hand around my waist, pulling me into the kiss. I kiss him back as if everything's normal.

But I saw what those folders on his desktop are. Every single one of them is labeled "Trinity."

10

KARL

The shoes pinch my feet, and my collar feels tight.

After living in flannelettes and jeans, the suit feels restrictive. The tie strangles me. I resist the urge to pull at my collar, and I keep my feet firmly planted.

"You failed to find my daughter, and now you want out of your dealings with me?"

Damon glares at me. He's reclining in his chair, his feet up on the desk and a whiskey glass in hand.

"I'm handing in my resignation, sir."

It pays to keep the niceties with Damon. He's a stickler for respect.

"You don't just resign from a company like mine, Karl."

There's a knot in my stomach. I knew it wouldn't be easy extracting myself from Fletcher Holdings, but it's the only way to keep my small town idyll with Trinity.

"I can manage my business holdings remotely until you find a replacement."

Damon slides his feet onto the floor and swivels his chair around to face me.

"You can't just walk away, Karl. You know that."

I swallow hard, perspiration gathering at the back of my neck. He doesn't just mean the warehouses I manage up north. He means turning a blind eye to the shipments that come through those warehouses.

"I've looked at your business proposal."

It's something I put to him a while ago, a legitimate business importing pet food. I've been wanting to get out of managing the Fletcher Warehouses for a long time. But I need his backing.

But that doesn't matter now. All I want is a quiet life with his daughter.

"I could make that happen for you."

It's tempting. A business of my own. A legitimate business.

"But how do I trust a man who failed to bring my daughter home?"

His gaze penetrates mine, and a bolt of fear goes through me. I'm not sure if it's a threat. Does Damon know I found Trinity but didn't bring her back?

I turn my hands up in a shrug, keeping my tone casual. "She just needs some time, that's my guess."

It's not a guess. It's what I know.

Ever since Trinity opened up to me about her family, she's confided more in me. She told me she never wanted to leave for good, just for enough time to have some space, figure out what she really wants to do with her life, not what her father has planned for her.

"She's had enough time. She needs to come home."

Damon slams his fist onto the table, making the whiskey glass jump. I freeze, not sure if he knows, if he's giving me a final warning to bring her back.

"Go." Damon dismisses me with a wave of his arm. "If you want out, I'll make that happen."

"Thank you, sir."

I should feel relief, but I'm uneasy as I leave Damon's office. It doesn't feel right. It shouldn't have been that easy.

In the men's bathroom, I take a moment, leaning on the counter and breathing hard. I'm not sure if Damon knows something or if I'm being paranoid.

I rip my tie off and undo my top button, letting my neck breathe.

I told Trinity I had to visit a client and would be away for a few days. But twenty-four hours without her, and I'm coming undone.

All I want to do is get back to her, back to her warm smile and soft eyes and sweet pussy.

I take my time in the bathroom, running over every transaction in the last few weeks.

There's no way Damon could have traced me. I've been careful. I've only used cash, and I've bounced my phone off VPNs so it's untraceable.

Perhaps I'm just being paranoid.

It's ten minutes later when I venture out to my car. I'm pulling out of the parking lot when a black BMW pulls in. I slow down to let it past.

My heartbeat catches when I see who's in the driver's seat. Sting. The man Damon uses to do his dirty work. The hitman.

Our eyes lock, and Sting's gaze is intense, boring into mine and full of darkness. Full of death.

Then he drives on to meet Damon.

Shit. If Damon's calling in Sting, then he knows.

I need to get to Trinity, and I need to get us the fuck away to somewhere safe.

11

TRINITY

y hands feel heavy in the soap suds as I wash my plate.

It's only been one day, less than twenty-four hours that Karl's been away to visit a client. I should be enjoying the time to myself. But without Karl, the house feels empty.

I'm torn between missing him and a growing suspicion that something's not quite right.

I went back to his house yesterday, once I knew he was safely out of town. I hunted everywhere for the laptop, but predictably it wasn't there.

I rack my brain looking for an explanation as to why he'd have files in my name. Of course he doesn't know Trinity is my name. It must be a coincidence.

Maybe Trinity is the name of some computer software. Or he's a massive fan of Carrie Moss and the Matrix. Or he has a sister called Trinity he's never mentioned. Or an ex-wife.

The thought makes my stomach drop.

I searched through Karl's house, looking for clues to

I'm not sure what. But the spare rooms were empty. The closets had nothing in them.

Each empty space made the jitters in my stomach grow.

His bedroom has a bedside table with an empty drawer and only one shirt hanging up in the closet. It's like he doesn't really live there, like this is all just temporary.

Car lights in the driveway get my attention, and despite my misgivings, there's a flutter of excitement when I recognize Karl's pickup.

He's not supposed to be home until tomorrow.

Even with this agitated lump in my stomach, I can't help the tremor of excitement that sweeps through my body and the smile that lights up my face.

I check my reflection in the hall mirror. If I'd known Karl was coming back tonight, I would have washed my hair.

Sweeping it behind my ears, I open the door just as he's about to knock.

The smile drops off my face when I see his expression.

"What's wrong?"

Karl closes the door behind him and wraps his arms around me, squeezing me so tight all the air goes out of me.

"You're all right."

He pulls back to look at me, his concerned gaze sweeping over my body. He's acting weird, and it's freaking me out.

"Of course I'm all right. What's going on?"

He brushes past me and peers out the kitchen window.

"We have to leave."

His voice is strong, commanding. He's not the easy-going Karl I've come to know. He lowers the blinds as if someone might be watching us.

"What's going on, Karl?" My voice comes out high pitched, giving away the fear that's inching into my heart.

He takes my shoulders in both hands and looks at me head on.

"Do you trust me?"

He looks concerned, and I want to say yes. But after the last few days, I'm not so sure. The laptop files, the empty house. There's something he's not telling me.

Karl sees my hesitation, and he asks me again.

"Do you trust me, Trinity?"

My name on his lips sends a bolt of fear through my heart.

Karl's eyes widen, and a nervous smile flickers across his lips.

"Trina. Do you trust me, Trina?"

He says it casually, like calling me Trinity was a simple mistake. But I know it wasn't.

He knows. He knows my real name. He knows who I am.

"What did you call me?" It comes out as a whisper, and I try to back away but he's gripping me by the shoulders.

"It doesn't matter what I called you. We need to leave. Now."

But it does matter. It matters a hell of a lot.

"Why, Karl? Why do we need to leave?"

He releases his grip on me, but the intense look he gives me is no less binding, riveting me to the spot.

"Can't you just trust me? We need to get out of here."

His words are scaring me. I don't know what's got him so spooked. But I can't leave with him, not until he explains himself.

"What's going on, Karl? Why did you call me Trinity? And why do we need to leave?"

He turns away in frustration, and I see a battle going on inside him. He runs a hand through his hair. Then, as he reaches a decision, he turns to face me.

"Because your father knows where you are."

My chest clenches, and I can't breathe. I take a step backward and bump up against the cupboards.

"How do you know about my father?"

My mind's racing. There must be a logical explanation. Maybe after what I told him about me he did some research.

But judging by the look Karl gives me, I know the truth is going to be worse.

"Because I work for him."

My chest feels heavy, and I can't breathe. I try to move backward, wanting to get away from him, but there's nowhere else for me to go.

"What do you mean?"

He looks miserable, and I almost feel sorry for him. Until he starts speaking.

"Your father sent me to find you."

"You're the thug?"

I move sideways along the bench, needing to get away from him. It's all been a lie. He lied his way into my life. He lied his way into my bed.

"As soon as I saw you, Trinity, I knew I couldn't send you home to your father."

"You lied to me." My shock has turned to anger. "You lied to me, Karl."

"Only because you wouldn't have wanted me if you knew the truth. I love you, Trinity. I've loved you since the moment I saw your photo. I was never going to bring you home to your father. I knew you'd be mine."

"You're speaking about me like I'm some kind of property. You're just as controlling as my father. I'm not his, and I'm definitely not yours, Karl. I ran away from a controlling man. Do you think I want to get involved with another one?"

"No. Of course not. That's why it had to be your decision. It had to be because you wanted it."

I think back to how we met, how I asked him out at the coffee shop, how I kissed him first, how I led him up to my bedroom.

My hand flies to my mouth.

It was all me. I wanted him, and I made the first move.

"Moving in next door, was that a coincidence?"

He hangs his head, and that's all I need to know.

"I wanted to be near you, Trinity. I have to be near you. I can't explain it, but my love for you, it's an obsession. I wasn't alive until I saw you, and having you in my life… It makes me whole."

I may have made the first move, but he engineered it all. He manipulated me.

The uneasiness—the fear that's been bunched up in my stomach—turns to anger.

"You engineered this whole relationship. I feel manipulated, Karl, treated like a fool. And those folders on your laptop with my name on them, what's in them?"

"Information. I was tracking you across the country, and when I found you, I kept tracking."

I'm reminded of what Jenny said about seeing him in his pickup. How I thought she must be mistaken because Karl was at home working.

"Do you even work in IT?"

He doesn't say anything, and his silence tells me what I need to know.

I sink to the floor. The man I thought I knew is nothing but a delusion.

"Get out, Karl."

He doesn't move. "We have to go. Your father's sent Sting. Do you know who that is?"

Sting, the hitman. It was finding out about Sting that made we want to leave my father's whole corrupt empire.

But how can I believe anything Karl says? He's probably just saying that to make me go with him.

"Get out."

The only sound is Karl's breathing, and I know he's waiting for me to stand up and go with him. But I don't look up. I can't look at him.

"I don't believe you, Karl, so get the fuck out of my house."

For a moment, there's silence. Then he steps quietly to the door.

"I'm sorry I caused you pain, Trinity. But I'm not giving up on you."

It's only once he shuts the door behind him that I let the tears fall.

1 2

KARL

*M*y legs ache from crouching, and the wet grass is starting to seep through the soles of my sneakers.

It's past midnight, and it's been over an hour since the light went out in Trinity's room. Watching from my window wasn't enough. If Sting arrives, I'll need to be on the ground to move fast. To keep Trinity safe.

My binoculars sweep over the front yard, the driveway, and the quiet street. A cat scampers from behind a bin and disappears down the side of a house.

Aside from that, there's no movement.

Trinity may not want anything to do with me, but that doesn't mean I'll abandon her. Even though it pained me to walk away, even though I felt physically sick leaving her, I also feel a sense of relief. She knows now. She knows my secret. It broke what we had, but at least she has the truth.

Lowering the binoculars, I scan the immediate area around me.

I hope Damon wouldn't kill his own daughter. But there's no telling what the man's capable of if he's mad enough.

A twig snaps behind me, and I whirl around, raising my gun.

There's a shape in the darkness. A man emerges out of the shadows. Sting. With his steel pointed straight at me.

He must have come through the back hedge. I set a tripwire, but the man's good. There's a reason why he's Damon's hitman.

"Are you here to kill me?"

I feel a surge of adrenaline. Sting keeps his gun trained on me, and I keep mine on him. We eye each other in the darkness, ready to shoot if the other one does, ready to both die together.

"Nothing personal. Boss's orders."

His voice is as hard as the expression on his face, and I wonder why he didn't shoot me in the back.

Sting takes a step toward me, and I calculate the distance. I could lunge for him, knock the gun out of his hand, but then what? I might get killed in the scuffle, and there'd be no one to bargain for Trinity's life.

"How did you find us?"

I'm stalling for time, hoping he edges closer, close enough to take a swing at him that I know wouldn't miss.

"The flowers you sent your ma."

Of course. The card from the flower shop. How could I be so stupid? I was careful to pay cash for every-thing, but the card must have had the name of the florist on it.

"She sends her regards, by the way."

My chest tightens as fear grips me. This brute has been to see my ma. "What did you do to her?"

"I wouldn't hurt an old lady." There's a hint of reproach in his voice as if I've offended some kind of hitman code of honor. "Your mom's fine. As far as she knows, I'm a concerned friend looking for your whereabouts."

It doesn't stop me from feeling uneasy. I don't like the thought of this killer visiting my mom.

"She makes good shortbread."

The thought of this beefcake sitting down over a cup of tea and shortbread with my ma makes the skin on the back of my neck stand up.

"She showed me her ribbons from the dog show. Very proud of those dogs, she is."

Sting's lip twitches, and I realize this is his attempt at humor, or at least being human. I may be able to use this if I keep him talking.

One thing's certain. He's not lying. My mom loves those dogs.

"Did she show you my football trophies?"

"Nope. Just the dogs."

I roll my eyes. Typical ma.

As Sting's been talking, his eyes haven't left mine. He may be enjoying this weird tête-à-tête, but he'd still kill me in a heartbeat.

"Listen. Damon just wants me. You hurt me, fine, but Trinity doesn't need to be harmed."

Sting shakes his head slowly as if I'm thick.

"Hurt you? You've been fucking the boss's daughter. You're lucky he only wants you dead."

Rage at his crass description of what me and Trinity share makes my blood hot, and I tighten my grip on the gun.

"It's not fucking. I love her." My voice is clipped, and I keep in the rage, but Sting doesn't seem threatened.

He tilts his head, and a softness passes across his face, an expression of curiosity and wistfulness. Then it's gone, and I wonder if I imagined it.

"Sorry, man. Nothing personal."

I catch movement out of the corner of my eye, a person creeping in the darkness behind Sting.

I keep my eyes on him, trying to keep his attention on me.

"I may have fucked up, but I'd do it all again to have those three weeks with Trinity. If I'm going to die tonight, at least I had that."

Sting gives me a curious look, but my words aren't for him.

"I'm sorry I fucked this up. I really am."

His eyes narrow suspiciously just as Trinity puts the gun to his head.

"Drop the gun, or I'll blow your fucking brains out."

Sting's eyes widen in surprise. But only for a moment. Then he's back to his hard-ass expression.

"You're not going to use that on me, Trinity."

"Try me."

Her voice is hard like I've never heard it before, and her expression is dark to match.

She looks badass dressed in tight black with a gun in her hand. She's not shy in how she holds it either. This is a woman who is used to holding steel, and I'll bet you anything she's used to shooting it too. Damon would have made sure of that.

Sting must know it too, but his voice remains calm.

"I'm not here to hurt you, Trinity. Just this asshole who's been lying to you."

She presses the barrel into his temple, and a flicker of fear passes through Sting's eyes.

"Call him that again, and I'll pull this trigger."

Sting keeps silent, which is wise for a man with two guns trained on him. I steal a glance at Trinity, but she's got her attention on Sting.

"If you kill Karl, I'll kill you and then I'll kill myself. You think that's what my daddy wants?"

"He wants you back. What are you protecting this guy for?"

Trinity flicks a quick glance at me. "Because I love him."

I feel it like a bolt to the heart. She loves me. Despite what I've done and who I pretended to be, she loves me.

"You're going to put the gun down. You're going to go back to my father and tell him I'm coming home but on my terms. Tell my father that I'm coming back with Karl, and if one hair on his head gets hurt, I will take myself and his unborn grandchild and he'll never see either of us again."

My mind reels at her words.

"You're pregnant?"

Trinity nods while keeping her gun on Sting.

"That's touching," says Sting, "but how do you think your daddy will take the news?"

"He already knows."

I glance at Trinity, and this time she looks at me. "I called my mom, told her everything. She was so happy to hear from me that she didn't care about any of it. Said she'd speak to my father. Mom can always bring him around."

Sting finally lowers the gun, and I lower mine.

"So, the hit's off?"

"It better fucking be."

Trinity lowers her gun, and I run to her, my hands going to her belly.

"When did you find out?"

"I did a test yesterday. I was going to tell you but…"

She shrugs, remembering the argument from yesterday.

"I'm so sorry, sweetheart, for how this all happened, for how I met you. But I've fallen in love with you. I'll take care of you and the baby."

"I don't need taking care of, Karl."

The words tear at my heart like a knife, but her hand goes to my cheek.

"I love you too, and I want to be with you. But I've been thinking. I wanted to get away from my family to figure out what I want to do. I think I know what that is now. I want to go back. I want to run some of the business, but legitimately. Dad taught me a lot about business, and I want to be involved but only if it's legit. No more dodgy deals, and no more hitmen."

We glance at Sting, but he's gone, faded into the shadows from whence he came.

Trinity's arms go around my neck, and I pull her close.

"Whatever you want, sweetheart. Wherever you want to be, I'll be right there with you. Always."

Four years later…

$\mathcal{I}$'m awoken by the feel of Karl's hand sliding over my belly and dipping between my legs. My hips push backward out of reflex, causing his hardness to nudge into my back.

I'm barely awake and already my body is responding to his touch, my pussy gushing wetness through my satin nightie as Karl's fingers stroke me into wakefulness.

"Morning, beautiful."

He nuzzles into my neck, the vibrations of his voice against my skin causing tiny prickles of pleasure and making goosebumps rise on my arms.

"Morning."

My words turn to moans as Karl's fingers wake up my center.

I push my hips more forcefully against his erection, loving the way it digs into my back.

Karl slides down the bed and flips my nightie up so his

cock rests between my ass cheeks. His hands rove over my body, grabbing my breasts and pulling me toward him.

It doesn't take long for my body to fully come alive and my pussy juices to flow. We glide together, his cock sliding between my folds until we can't stand it anymore.

Then his cock is in me, thrusting between my legs and filling up my pussy until my cries turn to moans.

Karl clamps a hand over my mouth. "Shhh, you'll wake the children."

The last thing I want is the kids to come bursting in, so I stifle my moans, biting into his hand instead.

The thought of being interrupted by our children brings a sense of urgency to our lovemaking, and I thrust myself onto Karl's cock, jerking my hips back so he plungers deeper.

His spare hand works my hard nub until the pressure builds, and I come hard on his dripping fingers.

He explodes at the same time, and I moan silently. Being forced to keep in the noise makes it more intense.

Afterwards, I roll over so we're nose to nose.

"Still the best way to start the day."

Karl kisses me gently, his stubble tickling my skin.

In the four years we've been together, I've never tired of waking up next to Karl.

We went back to confront my dad, taking our time traveling up the coast.

It took my dad a while to come around to Karl. He was angry at him for not bringing me home when he first found me, but once Dad realized I wasn't going to give Karl up, he gave us his blessing.

I started working for Fletcher Holdings again, but only on legitimate business. Almost losing two of his daughters was a wake-up call for my father. He wound down his non-legit business dealings.

Karl started his pet food importing business, and I had an idea of my own. Using Karl's warehouses and Dad's contacts, I'm now the owner of a flower distribution business.

I import flowers and distribute them to florists up and down the country, including Beautiful Blossoms which is still run by Aria.

My business has taken us on trips to see the tulip fields of Holland and the lavender fields of Provence. It's a lot to manage with two kids. But with my family for support and Karl's mom to help out, we manage.

The sound of the baby crying gets me out of bed, and I hurry to get him from his cot before he wakes his sister.

Too late. The bedroom door bursts open, and Callie trots in, her worn toy rabbit dangling from one hand.

She climbs into bed, and Karl makes room for her under the sheets. I bring the baby back into bed and feed him while Karl reads Callie a story.

It's the quiet family life we dreamed of.

We may have gotten here in an unusual way, but I know Karl would do anything for us, anything to protect us. And that makes me the happiest woman in the world.

THE HITMAN'S REDEMPTION

You always remember your first hit. But you don't expect to fall for his daughter...

For twelve years, I've been haunted by the girl with blue eyes flecked with amber. The girl who witnessed my first hit.

When our paths unexpectedly cross, I know I'll do whatever it takes to get close to her, even if it means pretending to be someone else. Someone better.

She must never know I'm the one who killed her father...

The Hitman's Redemption is Sting and Liberty's story, a sweet stalker, OTT instalove romance with a flawed hero and a curvy heroine who may just heal his heart.

Keep reading for an excerpt or visit:
mybook.to/TheHitmansRedemption

THE HITMAN'S REDEMPTION

CHAPTER ONE

Sting

The butt of the rifle presses against my cheek, its sharp metallic smell reminding me of Iraq.

It reminds me of when I was crouched on sand-covered rooftops, concealed and patient, covering my platoon as they cleared another war-damaged village.

My job was to wait, and when the enemy showed up, as they often did, I was ready.

As the platoon sniper, my job was an easy one: kill the enemy before they killed my soldiers.

But I'm not in Iraq, and the person on the other end of my sight isn't my enemy. They're someone else's enemy. I'm just the hired gun. The hitman.

There're only two people I work for. Damon Fletcher, who saved me from the streets when I was a homeless army vet with no future. And my other client, Markus Johnson, who fights the war on drugs with his own brand of vigilante justice. He gives me the details, and I don't ask questions. Any scum selling drugs to vulnerable people doesn't deserve to live.

A car turns onto the street, a black Mercedes with tinted windows.

In the fading light, I can just make out the license plate. This is my guy.

A sudden breeze sends a plastic bag tripping down the street ahead of the Mercedes. It rolls across the grass and catches on the edge of a broken fence, snagging between the twisted wires.

The car pulls up outside the only dark house on the street. Other houses have rectangles of yellow light with shapes moving behind them, families finishing their dinners and kids dragging their feet on their way to bed.

It's not a wealthy neighborhood. There's graffiti on the side of a garage and a couch dumped on the sidewalk, the long grass licking its edges.

Hard working families live here. Parents doing their best for their kids while working two jobs just to put food on the table.

It's the kind of neighborhood a man like the one I'm about to kill thrives on.

He's got no business driving in here with his Mercedes, making every young man on the street look at him with envy and every mother tut as fear grips her heart.

This community will be shocked when they learn their new neighbor is—soon to be *was*—a notorious drug dealer. The house has probably already been made into a lab. It's better to get this scum out of the neighborhood.

There'll be a scandal about the shooting, and mothers will worry if their kids are safe. But they'll be a hell of a lot safer than if this dirtbag had gotten a foothold in their community.

The drugs lab is just the start. Soon it would be recruiting bored teenagers looking to make a quick buck. Then there're the free samples. It's the vulnerable people in the community—the ones down on their luck, the ones with mental health problems, the army vets with nowhere to go, the single parents needing a few minutes of peace, the uneducated women who can only see one way to make a living and need a hit to block out their reality. Those are the ones men like this target. Those are the ones who'll pay the price if drug pushers are allowed to take hold.

The car stops, and the driver's door opens. My finger rests on the trigger of the gun. I've got to do it in the few seconds it takes him to walk from the car to his front door.

My body goes still, waiting for the right moment.

There's movement in the corner of my eye. I swing the sight around, and a girl on a bike comes into view.

What the hell is she doing out on her own in this neighborhood after dark?

She's got to be about twelve years old, her blond hair streaming out behind her as she rides.

The sound of a car door slamming snaps my attention back to the hit. He's out of the car and jingling his keys as he walks toward the house.

I've got to do it now.

The girl rides toward the man, and he turns to give her

a smile. She puts her foot on the ground and stops her bike to have a few words with him.

He's in my sights. If I pulled the trigger now, I'd get him right between the eyes. A clean hit. But I'd also get blood on the girl.

My mind goes back to another hit from twelve years ago, my first hit after Damon Fletcher pulled me off the streets and gave my life a new purpose.

I hesitated then.

Pulling a trigger when you're in the army and the guy on the other end is trying to kill your soldiers is one thing. But pulling the trigger in cold blood is another.

I hesitated, and the man ran. I chased him through the house, and there was a scuffle. We both ended up on the floor in the bedroom before I got my shot, his brain matter and blood spraying all over my clothes and face.

When he went still, there was a set of eyes watching me. A girl, about twelve years old, her eyes wide in shock, her pretty face splattered with blood.

I stared at her and she stared back, her dark eyes round and terrified.

There wasn't meant to be anyone else in the house. The intel Damon told me was wrong. I knew what he'd want me to do. He'd want me to tie up loose ends, to eliminate the girl.

But as we stared at each other, her eyes wide in terror, I knew in a heartbeat that I wouldn't harm her.

I pressed my fingers to my lips. "Shhh," I said.

The girl watched me, the terror giving way to curiosity. Her eyes were blue, with a fleck of amber in the left eye.

She started that day as a regular kid, probably thinking about what ribbon to wear in her hair and what music to play while getting ready for school. She ended that day with the blood of who I assumed was her father splattered across her face. Her life would never be the same again.

She grew up that day, whoever she was. I may have taken her father's life, but I took that girl's innocence. And that haunts me every single day, more than the numerous kills I've done since.

I won't do that to another little girl.

My finger eases off the trigger.

I don't know what she's talking to her new neighbor about, but I'm prepared to jump down there if he tries anything with her.

He smiles benevolently at the girl and reaches into his pocket. He pulls out a piece of candy, and her eyes light up as she takes it.

Didn't anyone warn her about taking candy from strangers?

The girl stuffs the candy into her mouth and gets back on the bike. She rides off, and the hit watches her as she turns into a driveway a few houses down.

He's got a sleazy smile on his face that makes me think there's another good reason for getting rid of this scumbag. No one should look at a little girl that way.

The girl dumps her bike in the front yard and pulls open the door. I hear gentle scolding from a woman inside. She's being chastised for getting home late, but at least she won't witness a murder tonight.

My target turns and begins to walk to his front door. I

follow him with my crosshairs. As soon as I hear the door shut behind the girl, I pull the trigger.

To keep reading visit:
mybook.to/TheHitmansRedemption

BOOKS BY SADIE KING

Sunset Coast

Underground Crows MC

Sunset Security

Men of the Sea

The Thief's Lover

The Henchman's Obsession

The Hitman's Redemption

Maple Springs

Men of Maple Mountain

All the Single Dads

Candy's Café

Small Town Sisters

Wild Heart Mountain

Military Heroes

Mountain Heroes

For a full list of titles check out the Sadie King website

www.authorsadieking.com